# Dot and the Dog

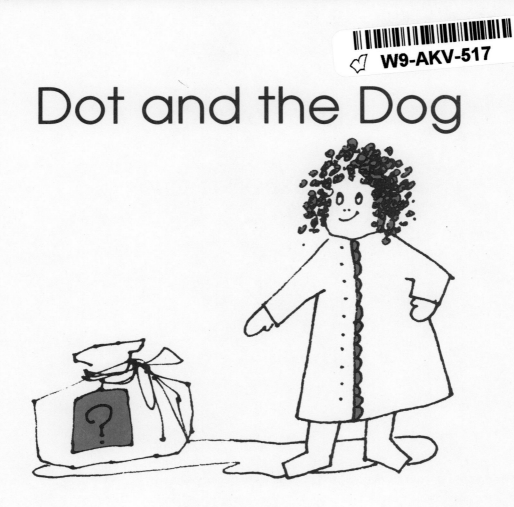

by Bobby Lynn Maslen
pictures by John R. Maslen

**Scholastic Inc.**
New York • Toronto • London • Auckland • Sydney • Mexico City • New Delhi • Hong Kong • Buenos Aires

# Book 6 adds:

## question mark

?

**Ask for Bob Books at your local bookstore, or visit www.bobbooks.com.**

No part of this publication may be reproduced, stored in a retrieval system, or transmitted in any form or by any means, electronic, mechanical, photocopying, recording, or otherwise, without written permission of the publisher. For information regarding permission, write to Scholastic Inc., Attention: Permissions Department, 557 Broadway, New York, NY 10012.

ISBN 0-545-02719-5

6 5 4 3 2 1          7 8 9 10 11/0

Printed in China
This edition first printing, September 2007

Dot had a bag.

The bag had a tag.

Is the bag hot?
The bag is hot.

Dot had a dog. The dog is Mag.
Mag got the bag. Dot got Mag.

Dot sat. Did Mag sit?
Mag sat on the bag.

Mag hid the bag.

Dot got Mag and the bag.

The bag had a hot dog.

The End

# Available Bob Books®:

**Set 1: Beginning Readers** — With consistent new sounds added gradually, your new reader is gently introduced to all the letters of the alphabet. They can soon say, "I read the whole book!®"

**Set 2: Advancing Beginners** — The use of three-letter words and consistent vowel sounds in slightly longer stories build skill and confidence.

**Set 3: Word Families** — Consonant blends, endings and a few sight words advance reading skills while the use of word families keep reading manageable.

**Set 4: Compound Words** — Longer books and complex words engage young readers as proficiency advances.

**Set 5: Long Vowel**s — Silent *e* and other vowel blends build young readers' vocabulary and aptitude.

# Bob Books® Collections:

**Collection 1** — Includes Set 1: Beginning Readers and part of Set 2: Advancing Beginners

**Collection 2** — Includes part of Set 2: Advancing Beginners and Set 3: Word Families

**Collection 3** — Includes Set 4: Compound Words and Set 5: Long Vowels